BEAUTY

SEP 26 2015

BEAUTY

BEAUTY

BEAUTY

Fashion

STYLE

TOP
10
RIGHT NOW

To Even, Iver, and Vilja
— *K. R.*

ANIMAL
Beauty

KRISTIN ROSKIFTE

EERDMANS BOOKS FOR YOUNG READERS

GRAND RAPIDS, MICHIGAN • CAMBRIDGE, U.K.

Every morning, people lined up outside the zoo, eager to get inside.

When they were finally allowed in, they ran in every
direction to see their favorite animals.

One day something strange happened. It all started when the elephant got hold of a fashion magazine. Curious, she turned page after page. "How to get rid of wrinkles," it said. *Oh? Get rid of wrinkles! Should I do that?* thought the elephant.
Luckily, the magazine was full of good advice.

"Elephant, what have you done?" asked the zebra.
"I just got rid of my wrinkles!" said the elephant. "I read about it in this magazine. Would you like to borrow it?"
"Sure!" said the zebra.

DAZZLE!

Trends from:
• New York
• Hollywood

LOOK YOUR BEST

TIPS!

"Never dress in horizontal stripes," the zebra read.
"I don't have anything *but* horizontal stripes," she said sadly.

Thank goodness for all the tips in the magazine.

"Is that really you, Zebra?" asked the panda.

"Yes, it's me. I've just stopped wearing horizontal stripes."

"Why?" the panda asked.

"They're unflattering, according to this magazine," said the zebra. "Do you want to see it?"
"Yes, why not?" Panda took the magazine and made himself comfortable.

"Are you bothered by dark circles under your eyes?" the panda read. He realized that he must be very bothered indeed, although he had never felt that way before. Fortunately, there were many ways to get rid of those dark circles.

Say GOODBYE TO
DARK CIRCLES
UNDER YOUR EYES

There is hope!

CELEBRITY TIPS!

"What kind of creature are you?" asked the snake.
"It's me — Panda," answered the panda. "I've finally
gotten rid of my dark circles! I found out about
them from a fashion magazine. Care to borrow it?"

"Snakeskin is unfashionable this year," the snake read with horror. *And here I've been slithering around thinking I look quite handsome. How mortifying!* He immediately checked the shopping websites the magazine listed.

MUST HAVES!

PARIS   NEW YORK   LONDON

YOUR GUIDE TO T... ON JUNGLE

CLOTHING

"Did you get stuck in something?"
asked the monkey.
"No, I'm just hooked on the latest trend. All the
celebrities are wearing leopard print now!"
"I'm not sure I understand," said the monkey.
"No, I didn't either. Read this magazine, and
you'll see what I mean."

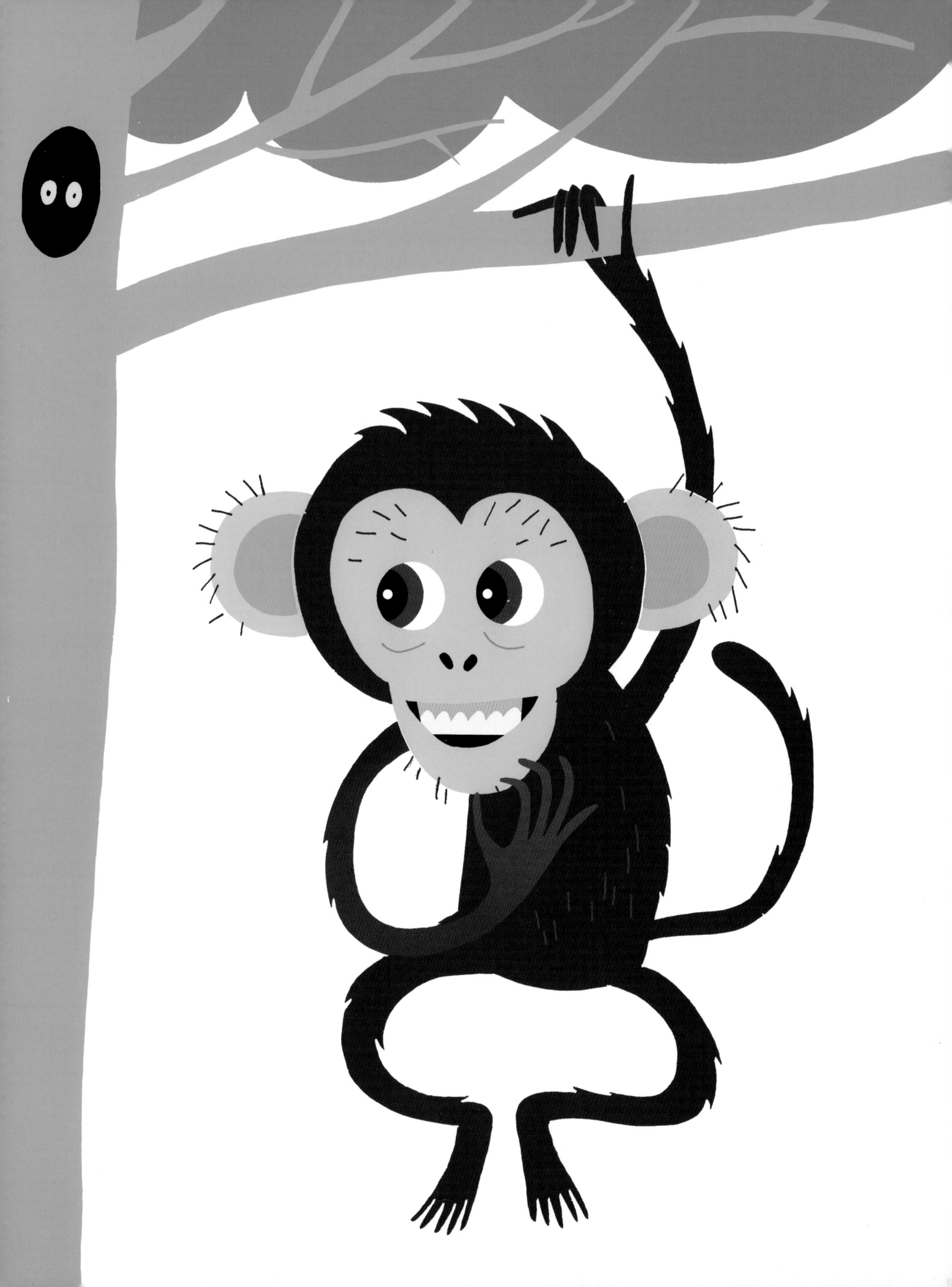

"Do you have unsightly hair on your face, arms, and legs?"
The monkey looked himself over. *Sure do*, he decided.
I'd better get started.

"Who are you?" asked the lion suspiciously.

"It's me — Monkey," said the monkey. "Can't you see that I have silky smooth arms and legs? And no more embarrassing hair on my face?"

"Yes . . . that's certainly quite a . . . change."

The lion was not completely convinced.

"I got some tips from this magazine. Would you like to see?"

"Do you have wiry and unruly hair?"
That's exactly what I have. Horror of horrors!
"Hair crisis!" the lion cried desperately.
There was only one thing to do.

HAIRDRESSER

OPEN

COME IN
FOR
A NEW
LOOK!

"What's happened to you, Lion?" giggled the flamingo.
"I went to the hairdresser and got a new hairstyle.
Here, borrow this magazine — maybe you'll learn
something too," said the lion.

"Have you been wearing pink since you were little?
Time to grow up!" the flamingo read.
I always wear pink! How hopeless!
What was I thinking?

"Who are you?" stammered the mouse.
"It's just me — Flamingo," the flamingo answered. "I've acquired a more grown-up style!"
"Oh? Maybe I ought to do that too," said the anxious little mouse.
"Yes, take this magazine. It's full of good advice."

"Are you a gray mouse?" the mouse read. *Yes, I sure am*, she thought sadly. According to the magazine, *nobody* wants to be a gray mouse.

"Eeek!" screamed the elephant, jumping up on a rock. "Take it easy, Elephant. It's only me — Mouse. I'm just the same, except I'm not gray any more. I'm a new me, all because of this fashion magazine. Would you like to borrow it?"

"No thanks!" said the elephant. "I've already read it. The magazine said I should use this face mask for my wrinkles. Now it's all stiff and itchy."

That afternoon the animals called a meeting. They gazed at each other curiously. They didn't know what to say. "We definitely look new, all of us," laughed the monkey. But the other animals weren't laughing.

The mouse piped up, "Shh! Do you hear that sound?"
"Yes, what a racket! Let's find out what's going on," cried
the elephant.

Soon they discovered a little boy crying.

"What's wrong, little friend?" asked the elephant.

"You're all so strange looking," sobbed the boy.

"Don't we look better?" asked Panda in surprise.

"Do you really think we looked better before?"
asked the lion, bewildered.

"Y-y-yes," cried the boy, "you have to be yourselves!"

The visitors gathered around, and all of them agreed:
the animals were best just as they were before.

"That is the best advice we've ever had," whinnied the zebra. And soon after, everything was back to normal in the zoo.

KRISTIN ROSKIFTE is an award-winning Norwegian author and illustrator. She has a MA in Illustration from Kingston University in England and has created several books for children.

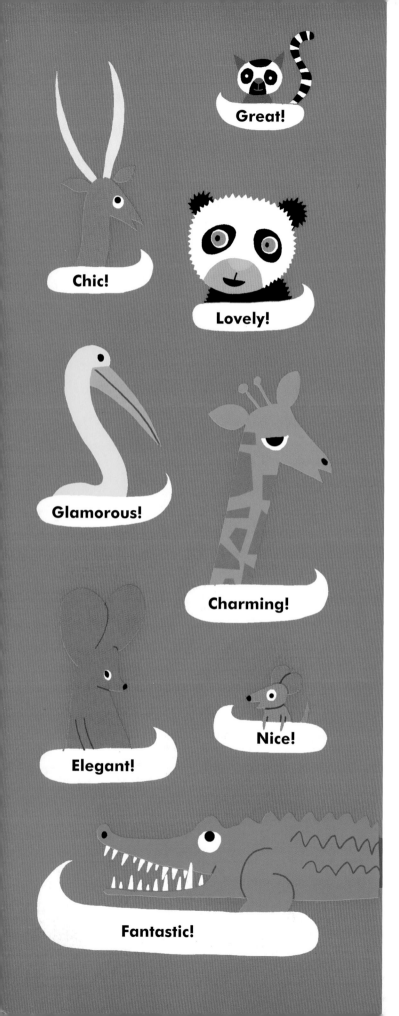

Great!

Chic!

Lovely!

Glamorous!

Charming!

Elegant!

Nice!

Fantastic!

First published in the United States in 2015 by
Eerdmans Books for Young Readers,
an imprint of Wm. B. Eerdmans Publishing Co.
2140 Oak Industrial Dr. NE
Grand Rapids, Michigan 49505
P.O. Box 163, Cambridge CB3 9PU U.K.

www.eerdmans.com/youngreaders

Originally published in Norway in 2012 under the title
Dyrenes Skjønnhet
by Magikon forlag, Fjellveien 48 A, Kolbotn, Norway
www.magikon.no
Translation by Jeanne Eirheim

Text and illustrations © 2012 Kristin Roskifte
© 2012 Magikon forlag
English language translation © 2015 Magikon forlag

Manufactured at Tien Wah Press in Malaysia

21 20 19 18 17 16 15   9 8 7 6 5 4 3 2 1

Text type was set in American Typewriter Light.
Display type was set in Humanist 521 BT and Curlz MT.

FSC
www.fsc.org
MIX
Paper from
responsible sources
FSC® C012700

Library of Congress Cataloging-in-Publication Data

Roskifte, Kristin, author, illustrator.
[Dyrenes Skjønnhet. English]
Animal beauty / written and illustrated by Kristin Roskifte.
pages cm
Summary: Zoo animals find a fashion magazine, pass it around, and start
to follow its advice.
ISBN 978-0-8028-5454-4
[1. Zoo animals — Fiction. 2. Beauty, Personal — Fiction. 3. Individuality —
Fiction.] I. Title.
PZ7.1.R674Ani 2015
[E] — dc23
EA2014048100

The ABC of Beauty

RIGHT NOW

MUST HAVE!

Celebrity tips: Forget natural beauty!

100%